Computer
Buttons

By Jill Carter and Judy Ling

buttons  computer

The **computer** said,
"Hello, hello.
Press my **buttons**.
I'm ready to go."

mother  octopus

A baby **octopus**
and a baby octopus's **mother**
get all tangled up
when they hug each other.

3

ears
mouth

eyes
nose

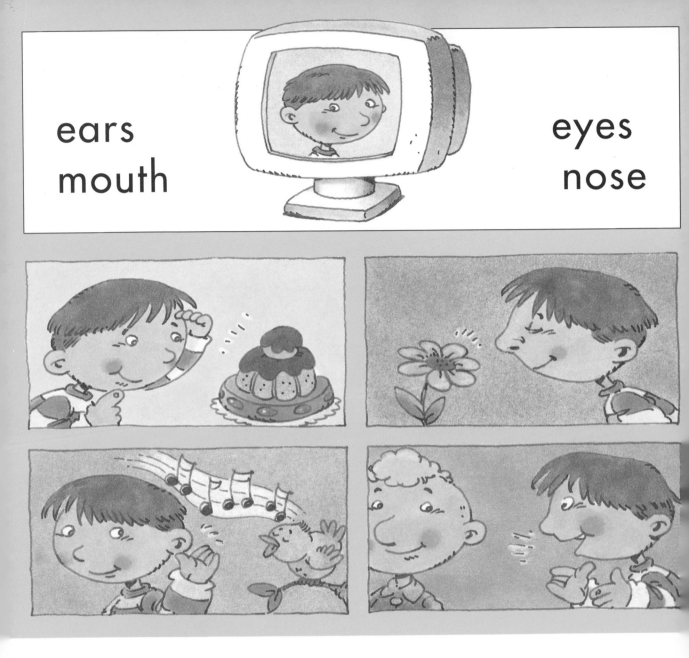

Your **eyes** are for looking,
your **nose** is for smelling,
your **ears** are for listening,
and your **mouth** is for telling.

bananas
pajamas

potatoes

Squishy **potatoes**
and squashy **bananas**
all slopped over
my new **pajamas**!

sky

water

Why does it rain?
Can you tell me why?
Why does **water**
fall out of the **sky**?

brother

hair
teeth

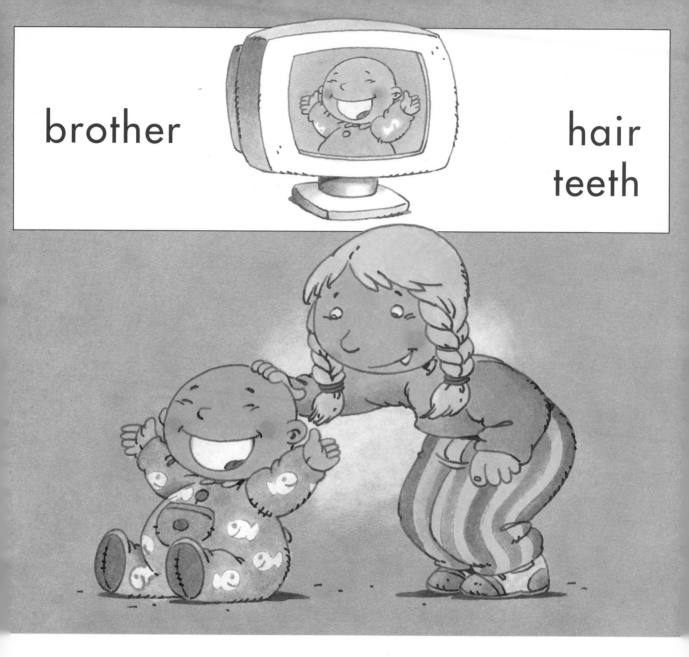

He has no **teeth,**
and he has no **hair,**
but my little **brother**
just doesn't care.

hat
smile

scarecrow
scarf

A **scarecrow** has a **hat**
and a brightly colored **scarf**.
He never has a **smile**,
and he doesn't even laugh.

8

land

sand
waves

Great big **waves**
crashing on the **sand**.
Great big **waves**
eating up the **land**!

animals
sea

cans

Cans of strange **animals**
zooming around the **sea**.
Where are they going?
What could they be?

butterflies  flamingos
flies

Flamingos, flies,
and **butterflies**—
they can fly,
but why can't I?

bath
bus

books

Books can make you cry.
Books can make you laugh.
You can read them anywhere,
on the **bus** or in the **bath**.

beanstalk
giant

bed
Jack

When **Jack** climbed up
the **beanstalk**,
what do you think he saw?
A sleeping **giant** on his **bed**.
Snore, snore, snore.

13

bed
head

books
table

Can you set the **table**?
Can you make your **bed**?
Can you balance **books**
while standing on your **head**?

14

clothes washing machine Dad

When **Dad** washed my **clothes** in the **washing machine**, they went in white, and they came out green.

Dad
Mom
noise

day
night
toys

"Pick up your **toys**!
Don't make that **noise**!"
Every **night** and every **day**
that's all **Mom** and **Dad**
can say.